Buford

BUFORD

A NOVEL

Buford

BUFORD

THE MAN
WITH NO EYES

Jerry W. Burns

Buford

BOOKS BY
JERRY W. BURNS

Preacher's Kid
Listen to the Music
Good Grief
Along the Journey
Mariah
Burns-Craft
All the Marbles?
Friends
Buford

Chili Publishing
Dallas, Texas

Dedication

To

Brian

Julie

Ethan

Aidan

Carson

Kendall

Patrick

Aimee

Jay Middlebrooke

Don Umphrey

David Fleer

Denise Guardino Urell

Judy Skelton

Paul Campbell

Earl Young

Sam and Sadie

Buford

IN THE
BEGINNING

A DIFFERENT
WAY OF
SEEING

Buford

Even though I was now in serious trouble for going downtown in our West Virginia city alone and without permission, I was temporarily put at ease by the wonderful, baritone voice of Mr. Buford.

Any person who ever heard that wonderful, clear, happy and melodious voice would never think of Mr. Buford as "The Man with No Eyes," but an educated, sensitive, warm person who knew so many answers to the great questions of life

Buford

THE

GOSPEL

BIG TOP

Listen before you speak.

We use more than

eyes to see.

We only hear what

we want to hear.

Buford

He was the largest man I had ever seen. I was not afraid of him, as he seemed so gentle and kind, but I was simply overwhelmed by his size. My father and grandfather were both big men, perhaps the largest and most important men I had ever known – until I saw that big man on Jefferson Street in the town where we lived in the northern mountains of West Virginia in the late 1940s.

I slowly walked to his newsstand on the sidewalk next door to the Central Cafe, where we often went after church and had root beer floats. Perhaps I should explain that a little better. What I should say, it was where we went for lunch. The grown-ups always ordered the "Blue Plate Special," the lunch of the day, but all I remember are the root beer floats. After all, I was just an elementary school kid, and that is the way kids think. They always think of the desert first.

While we were waiting for the floats after our lunch, Dad took some change from his pocket and asked me if I would like to go to the little newsstand outside, on the sidewalk in front of the Central Café' and buy the Clarksville Sunday newspaper—something he always did after lunch each Sunday.

I gladly took the change, excited that Dad trusted me to go alone to purchase the paper. I walked slowly toward the big man. I was walking as quietly as I could and knew the man could not see me, but instantly he turned toward me, smiled, and said good morning young man, did you go to church this morning?

Nervously, I put the change in the

little tin cup, one coin at the time. The man smiled broadly as he always did and said, you paid me a dime too much. Not knowing the proper thing to say, I replied, I'm sorry, I just gave you what my father gave me to buy the paper.

He threw back that enormous head and laughed gently, softly as he said, tell Reverend, I appreciate his business and hope he is having a good Sunday.

I had often seen blind people with seeing eye dogs and red and white canes but had never seen someone with no eyes at all; just empty holes where eyes should have been. That sounds frightening, but the big man on Jefferson Street was so big, soft-spoken and kind I never thought of him as deformed or bad looking. I even thought he was a nice-looking man; someone you might be drawn to in a crowd. There was just something different and special about that big man.

During the next several years I was to learn that many things made Buford different, different in a wonderful way. He was a philosopher among many other things, but his kindness and wisdom were the things I would always remember, and of course his lessons for life.

My father was the pastor of the Main Street Christian Church in Clarksville and was well known in town as he was a friendly man and loved people – all kinds of people. When I went downtown with Dad, people always spoke to us, and they called him different things, even though he didn't care for titles.

Some called him preacher; others called him pastor or minister. But the big man who sold newspapers on Jefferson Street always called him Reverend.

Dad didn't like that name and often told people that only the Lord should be called Reverend, but he seemed pleased when the big man selling newspapers called him Reverend.

I could tell that Dad liked the big man very much. He began each day with a walk downtown, which was just a few blocks from where we lived.

He often stopped at the little cafe and had a cup of coffee with local citizens and always stopped at the little newspaper stand and bought the local newspaper and sometimes a magazine or out of town newspaper.

My Father

My father always stood out. He was a tall man, always immaculately dressed in a three-piece suit with tie and hat. I have often told people about his appearance. He loved the great outdoors, hunting and fishing.

My father believed that a minister of the Lord should be well dressed and have good manners. When my father went fishing, he wore a tie and a plaid, wool, Pendleton shirt-jacket.

That Sunday when I went alone to buy the paper, I wondered how the big man knew who I was. The big mystery was how the man knew how much money I had put in the cup. I had many disturbing thoughts that day. Before that Sunday, I had never thought a great deal about the big, blind man. He was just a friend of my father who sold newspapers. But all of that was about to change.

That day was different; the big man made a lasting impression on me which changed my life. I have thought throughout my adult life, that I would write a book about Buford and the many, wonderful life's lessons he taught me.

It was difficult to sleep that night, but the next day was a school day, and life for a young kid is full of wonder and exciting things with little room left to dwell in the world of adults.

When I arrived at Pierpont Elementary School that Monday, all the kids in my class were talking about the big circus which had come to town, it was quite a coincidence that the circus, complete with the big top tent, wild animals and clowns was coming at the same time my father was planning to conduct a gospel meeting in his big canvas tent.

.

As kids are prone to do, the kids at Pierpont got the two tents confused in their thinking and were talking about Dad's tent as a circus tent. The rumor spread that Tim's dad had a circus tent.

Tim – that's what all my friends called me when I was young; however, my full name is Timothy Dwight Harrison. I have always been upset with my name – at least until now. I always thought it unfair that parents got to stick a name on us that lasts forever. It would be much better, I thought, if they would wait a few years and let us kids try out a few names until we found one that suited us.

No one except my father called me Timothy. Mom said I should be proud of that name because my father named me after one of his favorite young preachers in the Holy Scriptures. My mother, a very practical person, told me that she preferred to call me Tim. She reasoned that the young preacher called Timothy in the King James Version of scripture might someday be known as Tim in later, more modern translations of the scriptures.

Even though I was unhappy with Timothy, I hated being called Tim, because it always reminded me of "Tiny Tim" in the Christmas story of Mr. Dickens that Mom read to my older brother and me each Christmas. I did not want to be "Little Tim," or "Tiny Tim" or "Timmy," because I wanted to be a big man like my grandfather, who was the biggest man in the mountains of Tennessee where he was born. He was the biggest man I had ever known until I learned about the big man at the newspaper stand on Jefferson Street.

Dad managed to negotiate with the circus manager and have the circus elephant raise his big canvas tent on a vacant lot just down the street from the circus site. The tent canvas was raised by harnessing the elephant to a steel cable which was threaded through a series of pulleys at the top of the center pole of the tent. That was the day the elephant raised the Gospel Big Top in Clarksville, West Virginia.

How many fathers own a real tent, just like a circus tent? That is one of the great mysteries of my life. I have often said I would give anything to have just one more day to sit in a comfortable place with a jug of iced tea and ask my father questions and listen to the stories of his life.

I can assure you that one of the first questions I would ask is this, Dad, where in the world did you get that circus tent and how much did it cost?

Every time we moved, which was about every 3 or 4 years, one of my father's problems was how to move the tent. Please be assured that I'm not writing about a family-camping tent, but an honest-to-goodness circus-style canvas tent, that would hold 300 to 400 folding chairs. There were side curtains all around to make the interior water and wind resistant in inclement weather. Strings of yellow lights were strung throughout the dome of the tent as most revivals were held at night.

During a revival, there were always teenagers, boys, and girls who were not too interested in that old-time religion, but each other. Invariably, before the evening service—which always started late because of the summer heat—the teenage boys made sure the yellow lights were not working in the back, assuring there would be a very dark area at the rear of the assembly. All the teenagers knew the area would be dark and they could do what teenagers do when it is dark.

When I was growing up, it was simply a given that my father owned a tent, a very large tent. It was simply part of who we were. I remember the tent from the time I was 5 or 6 years old and the last time I remember seeing it was the autumn I went off to my freshman year of college.

That old "gospel big top," like an old man, kept shrinking through the years. During my last year of high school, Dad put the remains of the tent up in a field behind our home, the pastor's parsonage, and it remained up for the entire year. Dad would have classes in the tent for young boys training to be pastors and had parties and social activities for his congregation.

T o complicate things further; another religious revival was taking place the same week as Dad's tent revival meeting and the circus. The revival downtown, in a multiple-use auditorium, was announced as a faith healing revival with a famous faith-healing pastor from California. Dad, being a very conservative minister, didn't have much confidence or respect for the freewheeling faith healers who seemed more intent on passing the contribution buckets. It seemed to me that there are always people in every position in life who are ready to pounce on simple people and take advantage of their simple goodness.

The faith-healing revival seemed to be getting all the attention that week in

Clarksville, even more than the circus. They had signs and billboards posted all over town, promising to heal disabled people and even restore sight to the blind. The revival people from California were putting on quite a show and getting a lot of attention in our town, not to mention, collecting a lot of money.

That Monday, Dad made his usual walk downtown. He was quite a sight. He never went out of the house unless he was dressed up. In those days he always wore a double-breasted suit, stiff white shirt, silk tie and dress hat – straw in the summer and wool in the winter.

He went to the cafe for coffee, where everyone was talking about the faith-healing revival. Dad's coffee-drinking friends wanted to know what he thought about the faith-healing meeting and the slick people from California who were collecting a lot of money. Dad didn't comment much, as he never liked to talk about people if he could not say anything good.

Clarksville, W.VA.

After coffee, Dad walked to the newspaper stand to buy the morning paper from the big, blind man who said, good morning Reverend, what do you think about the big faith-healing meeting? It's causing quite a stir in our town. Dad replied that he thought the whole scheme was about making money, not bringing hope and change into people's lives. Dad said, Buford, have you thought about going? After all, they are claiming to heal the crippled and restoring sight to the blind.

The big, kind man smiled and softly replied that he didn't have much confidence in the healing claims. After a while, Dad, with a twinkle of mischief in his eye, suggested that Buford attend the meeting one night as the auditorium was just a block from his newspaper stand.

Buford told Dad, you know as well as I do Reverend that I will never have vision again. I see and hear things you will never experience. Dad gently laughed and agreed with his big friend.

The big man suddenly said, Reverend, I think you might have a good idea. I think I *will* go to the meeting one night and see what they do when I walk in. If you have coffee with me soon, I'll let you know what happens. It would be a while before Dad learned about Buford's adventure at the faith healing meeting, as he was busy that week with his tent revival.

At Pierpont School that Monday, Ms. De Vita slapped the ruler on the corner of my desk to get my attention; it seems I had been daydreaming and not paying attention. I had been busy thinking about sounds, money and tin cups. I just couldn't quit thinking about that big man at the newspaper stand – Buford. How did he know exactly how much money I had dropped in the cup yesterday when Dad sent me to the stand to buy the paper? And what concerned me was how he knew who I was. After all, he could not see anything.

I had been thinking about all this with my eyes shut at my desk, trying to understand what it must be like to never see. I jumped from my desk with a start when the ruler hit my desk! All the kids laughed, and Ms. De Vita demanded that I pay attention to the lesson.

Ms. De Vita was a good teacher, I suppose, but all I remember is that she was a strict disciplinarian. She was so strict that we could not go to the bathroom until it was time for all the students to go. Then we had to line up in the hall and go into the bathroom one by one – silently. I have never forgotten the day she heard someone talking and thought it was me.

I tried to explain to Dad that I was not talking in the bathroom line and did not deserve the spanking Ms. De Vita gave me. I was pleading my case because of the strict rule Dad had which assured me if I got a spanking at school, I would also receive one at home for good measure. And Dad's punishment was something to be avoided if possible.

My punishment was always carefully planned. Dad would take his time and explain why he had to administer the corrective measures in my development. Then we went to the garage where his old thick leather razor strap was administered in support of my moral education.

When the ruler hit my desk that Monday, Ms. De Vita demanded, Tim Harrison, why are you sleeping during the lesson? But Ms. De Vita, I stuttered, I was not sleeping. I just had my eyes closed; trying to see what it is like to be blind. To that response, the class laughed.

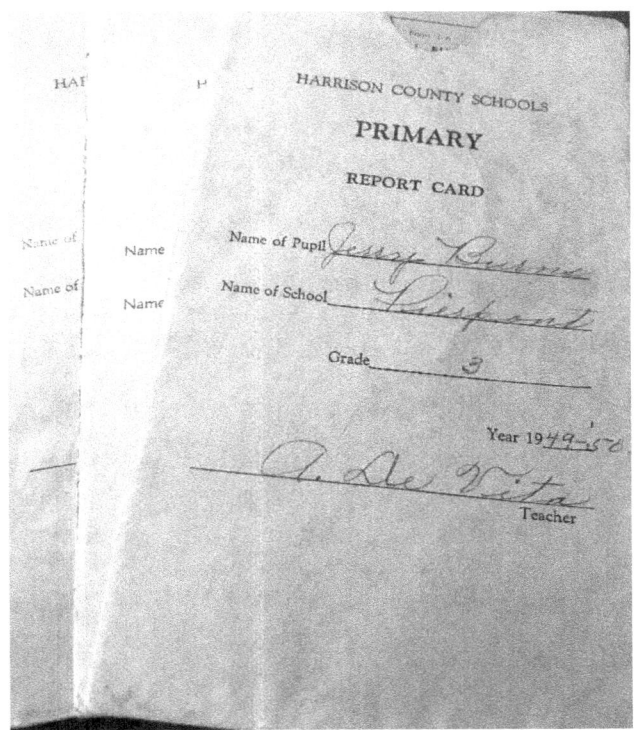

Things begin to get out of control until Ms. De Vita slapped her hands and demanded that we be quiet and pay attention to the lesson. I had to suspend my experiment in vision deprivation momentarily.

I now know that the effort of a kid to try and understand the situation of other people and sympathize with their handicaps is a valuable lesson to learn at any age. It always seems that children are quicker to overlook shortcomings in others, and not let physical and emotional characteristics dictate how we relate to people

That was long in the past. Now, most of those I knew and loved—but did not understand—are gone, but I think about them more and more now, and I still reach out to them. I try to understand them as I try to understand who I have become. Buford was never healed. When he went to the faith-healing service, they handed out numbered cards at the door. When the time came for the healing prayer at the end of the service, they asked for those with certain numbers to come forward. Buford's number was never called.

Buford, the big man, was well educated and lived with his braille books and hundreds of records of classical music. He heard and understood things I never knew. As a child, I accepted and loved him, but now I am old, and those I love don't always understand who I have become. But I still reach out to them.

THE BIG
YELLOW
BUS

You don't need
all the marbles,
just enough to play
the game.

If you want to learn,
learn to listen,

Buford

P erhaps you have seen the commercial. I didn't think too much about it at the time. I didn't even notice the sponsor or the intended message, but this morning while reading *The Weight of Glory* by C. S. Lewis, the image of that commercial suddenly appeared. I will try to describe the scene.

A young boy, perhaps 10 or 12, gets on the yellow school bus and starts down the aisle when suddenly about midway a tough-looking kid grabs our boy by the arm and snarls, See you after school!

The message is all too clear – the tough kid is picking a fight. The boy— completely dejected, with head down— trudges toward the back of the bus, and with a sigh, flops down on the back row. We can all sympathize with the thoughts going through his mind. All of us can relate to the bullies of the world.

Bullies, bad people, war, poverty, ignorance, doubt, fear, and all the ills of life can be summed up in the dejection and the sight of the young boy. We've all been there and can relate – every day it seems.

The bus continues. Suddenly the young boy looks across the aisle and sees the biggest kid; he has ever seen in his whole life. Why he is so big, he takes up the whole bench, meant for two. The big kid smiles and says, Hi, can we be friends?

Ah, the young boy's eyes lighted up with a twinkle and plastered on his young face is a smile, with no mistaking the meaning behind it – I'm saved; I can't wait!

The Big Kid on the back row of the bus—that we're all bouncing along on in life is looking out for his friends. He's there for us always, and more than anything wants to be friends with everyone on the bus, even the tough, mean kids. But they can't relate.

I turned back to the C. S. Lewis book and read, "… to be loved by God, not merely pitied, but delighted in as an artist delights in his work or a father, a son – it seems impossible, a weight or *burden of glory* which our thoughts can hardly sustain. But so, it is."

The Big Kid is sitting on the back row watching how we treat each other.

I first learned about the diverse community of kids riding on that yellow bus when I was six or seven; when we were living in Clarksville, West Virginia. Like many communities in the confined spaces of the industrialized northeast, our small neighborhood was a community of different nationalities, cultures and religious beliefs. My world was limited to that small community, and it was a great experience to be part of the daily drama played out on the tiny stage of that colorful neighborhood.

Those carefree days and the diverse group of kids was one of the greatest experiences of my childhood. It was a lesson on how to get along and how to treat people.

We thought nothing of our differences: origin, religion or race. Even our age seemed to make little difference, as we all played together – from 6 to 16. Sure, we fought, argued and had our differences, but we never had any problem large enough to keep us apart the next day.

My group of buddies included two teenage kids of Greek immigrants who lived behind us. Their father was a clergyman in the Greek Orthodox Church. On one side of the minister's parsonage where we lived, was the child of a Jewish family and in the home next to us on the other side, a kid whose Catholic family was from Italy. Two or three houses down the street lived one of my best friends, Teddy, the smallest kid in the neighborhood – a bright and happy young kid. Teddy was a different color than most of us, but no one cared or even thought about the difference. Teddy was probably the best kid in the neighborhood, with the biggest heart. There were girls in our group of playmates, but it seemed that the only game they liked was *spin the bottle.* If you do not remember that childhood party game, you have forgotten something important

After all the years, I can still see that group of kids, playing together in peace and harmony every day until after dark—playing kick the can in the middle of the street. I often wonder what each of those wonderful kids did through the years after we left the mountain state.

nd now, almost 70 years later as I write about these adventures, once again, living alone, I find myself in a wonderful diverse community of people where I now live, in a busy Metroplex of almost six million people. The children of this community in the year 2018 are my friends. They are all different nationalities, races, and colors, but don't tell them, because they all accept each other, at least until the adults of the world teach them differently.

I lost my wife of 51years—almost two years now, and If not for the love of the children of this community, and the love they give to me, I would be lost. Every day as I pull into my parking space, the kids come running, calling my name, Tim, Tim. It is quite a sight, seeing me trying to walk to my apartment door with sweet kids hanging onto my legs. We read in sacred scripture, let the little children come to me. Unless you become as one of these children, you will not enter the kingdom of heaven.

In Clarksville, West Virginia, we all played together every day until dark. We played kick-the-can in the alley and shot games of marbles anywhere we could find a small, level area of smooth, packed dirt.

Our marble games began by drawing a small circle in the dirt with a stick – a circle from one to two feet in diameter. We each dropped a marble in the center and then tried, with many arguments, to determine the order of shooting, especially who would shoot first.

Each kid, in turn, would kneel in the dirt and place his shooting hand at the edge of the circle. The "shooter" marble was held in the crook of one's index finger and shot or flipped by the thumb toward the group of marbles in the circle.

The object was to hit the group of marbles, or a single marble, hard enough to cause a marble to roll out of the circle. If your shooting caused a marble to roll out of the circle, it was yours to keep. There was no mistake as to whom each marble belonged. We knew our marbles better than we knew our school lessons. Another important thing: no one ever touched another kid's "shooter" marble. They were special. If you ever lost your "shooter" marble, you were really "down on your luck."

Those beautiful glass marbles were our treasure and pride; They were our bargaining strength and collateral. Like our fathers putting wallets and keys in their pockets each morning, we started our day of adventure by putting our marbles in our pants' pocket – that is, if we ever took them out.

We were never without a pocket full of marbles, except perhaps at church. Even then, we probably at least had our "shooter." We were always ready for a game: at school on the playground at recess, walking to school or on the way home. Anywhere there were a couple of kids and a spot of smooth earth a game would quickly materialize. We were always looking to add another marble to our collection of wealth.

That Friday afternoon, after Ms. De Vita slapped my desk with the ruler, I was more determined than ever to understand what it was like to have no eyes like my big friend Buford. Kids instinctively sympathize with others who are different, sick, injured or simply looking for a friend like the Big Kid on that yellow school bus.

It was not far from our house to downtown Clarksville, but I had never been allowed to walk down there alone. But today was somehow different; I did not stop to try to find kids to play marbles with, because more important things were on my mind.

I could not quit thinking about the big man Buford, who had no eyes but could see things. Even at that early age, I had an unquenchable desire to know certain things. The things I wanted to know then were just as important as the things I want to know now as an old man.

Even though I knew I might be in trouble, I kept walking that afternoon until I was on the street where Buford had his newsstand.

That decision was one of the most important decisions I have ever made. That day was the beginning of a unique and wonderful friendship and learning experience that would change the course of my life for the better. I will never forget that day. I have wondered many times through the years why I kept walking that day until I was on Jefferson street where Buford had his newspaper stand.

When I saw the big man, my heart began to beat faster I could not suppress the excitement I felt. When I got closer to the newsstand, I walked very slowly and quietly; I was amazed and in shock when Buford threw back that big head of his, laughed, and said good afternoon to the son of the Reverend.

I stood speechless, just staring at the big man. Finally, Buford said, Tim, what are you doing in town alone? And then he laughed even harder. The big man said, Tim I'm glad to see you, but I hope you have permission to come downtown. By my silence, he knew that I did not. <u>Then Buford said, Tim, I guess you know</u> that I'll have to tell the Reverend the next time I see him, but I think it will be ok.

I finally got up enough courage to speak to Buford. I said, Mr. Buford how did you know that it was me because you can't see. Buford laughed again and said

Tim, simply because I have no eyes, does not mean I cannot see. And then I learned one of the most important lessons in my life.

Buford said, Tim, close your eyes real tight and be very quiet for a few moments. I stood as quietly as I possibly could with my eyes squeezed tight. Even though I was fascinated by Buford, I was still intimidated by him. And so, I stood there with my eyes as tightly closed as possible.

Finally, Buford said Tim what do you hear? With a tiny quivering voice, I said, Mr. Buford, I hear cars passing by, and I hear horns honking. Buford quietly said is that all you hear Tim? I said yes sir. Finally, he told me to open my eyes.

Buford put his hand on my shoulder and gently said, with your eyes closed you heard cars and trucks. The things that you hear paint an image in your mind of what you are hearing. You heard noises that painted a picture of cars and trucks on your mind. During that time that your eyes were closed mine were also. But I also heard something that reminded me of beautiful flowers. While your eyes were closed, you heard cars and trucks.

During that same time, with my eyes closed, I heard a cricket, and that made me think of beautiful flowers. So, Tim, you heard sounds that made you think of cars and trucks. I heard sounds that made me think of beautiful flowers.

After finally getting up enough courage to speak, I looked up at Buford and said, But Sir, I didn't hear any crickets. I don't see any crickets; besides, I thought they lived in the grass.

Then Buford took my hand, and we walked over to a storefront that had a flower box. Buford said, Tim, look in that flower box carefully. I did as he told me and was greatly surprised when I saw a big fat cricket. I said Mr. Buford, how did you hear that cricket?

That was the first, and probably one of the most important lessons I learned from the big man with no eyes. He taught me the valuable lesson that throughout life we listen and hear what we want to hear. Oh, I know that most people would respond and say that they hear everything. But that is not true.

When I became a grown man, I still had to relearn that lesson from Buford. I call it selective hearing. The lesson teaches that we cannot hear if we are busy thinking about what we want to say. We can only hear when we are silent. Listening is the most difficult trait to learn.

Buford

THE WEALTHIEST KID IN TOWN

Enough is all you need.

Life is not about
who has the most
marbles.

You will never own anything
until you are willing to give it to
someone.

Buford

F or a short period I was a very wealthy kid. I was easily the richest kid in Clarksville, and it went to my head. I was smitten with the sin of pride that my Dad talked about in his sermons at church. I was wealthy because I owned "all the marbles." I was primed for a downfall despite the Biblical warning to not put our trust in treasures on earth, where thieves break through and steal. I should probably explain how I became so wealthy at the tender age of six.

Glass and pottery manufacturing were an important industry in West Virginia, due to abundant natural resources used in glass and pottery production: sand, clay, coal, gas, and timber. China, pottery, fine crystal and a variety of glass products were produced in factories near where we lived in the northern part of the state.

Dad became friends with an executive of a factory in Clarksville where glass products including marbles were produced. It was the only glass factory in the United States at that time producing beautiful glass marbles. Dad often visited his friend at the factory. They had coffee in the executive's office and walked through the plant together. Dad enjoyed making friends in all the various communities where he was a minister. He was truly interested in people, their vocations and interests.

After one of his visits to his friend's glass factory, Dad asked me to walk out to the garage with him. He said he had something to show me. I was sure hoping the item he wanted me to see wasn't his leather belt, the belt; he used to administer punishment when I had done something necessitating corrective measures in my attitude and demeanor. He believed in keeping such administrative activities private – hence the garage.

This trip to the garage was wonderful, for there in the corner was the greatest treasure I had ever seen – a great wooden chest filled with gleaming, gorgeous, glass marbles of many sizes, designs, and colors. Now, this was no ordinary gift. The chest itself was a work of art. It was a large chest about the size of a crate used to ship fruit to grocery stores and had been skillfully crafted from hardwood. It was so heavily laden that Dad had a difficult time picking it up, and he was a big man.

The ample space of the chest was filled with extraordinary marbles, not the ordinary solid-color opaque marbles that come with games like Chinese checkers. These were crafted of clear globes of quality glass, surrounding colored ribbons, spires and flowing designs within.

To a kid of my age, that wooden crate, filled with hundreds, perhaps thousands of beautiful glass marbles, was the equivalent of a million- dollar certificate of deposit in the adult's world.

I was wealthy, but my simple, nice, ordinary world was about to change. Kids soon noticed I had more marbles than usual, and they were much more beautiful than their well-used old marbles. Word leaked out that I had an enormous stash of quality marbles and many of my friends became jealous and didn't want to shoot marbles with me. I was not happy.

A few days after Dad brought home the crate of marbles, we went out of town on an overnight trip to Bethany, West Virginia. Bethany was a beautiful mountain town and the home of Alexander Campbell, one of the founders of the religious Restoration Movement of the19th century. Dad was a student of the movement, and we went to Bethany many times while we lived in the state. We visited the Campbell home, library, cemetery and Bethany College that Campbell founded in 1840.

When we returned home to Clarksville, as you might have guessed, our garage had been broken into, which wasn't difficult as it was never locked. The beautiful wooden chest was still there, but almost empty. Instead of hundreds of marbles, there was only a handful left in the bottom – a pitiful sight.

In the days that followed, it seemed that all the kids in the neighborhood had pockets full of new marbles. There wasn't just a single thief, but all the kids had stolen marbles. It turned out that on the day we were out of town all the kids in the neighborhood, led by the oldest kid, lined up to fill their many pockets from my chest. I was crushed and despondent.

I told my friend, Buford, about the theft of my marbles. I was shocked when he didn't show a lot of sympathies but simply said, life is not about who has the most marbles, but about having good friends and people to love. The big blind man then said I believe you will see your marbles again. But remember, we don't own anything until we give it away. It would be a few days before I learned the full intent of this lesson.

Early the following Saturday morning, I was looking out my upstairs bedroom window and was surprised to see Teddy sneaking into our garage. I stared in disbelief for a few minutes and then saw Teddy coming out of the garage, running quickly out of sight between two houses. What could he possibly want, I thought, the marbles were all gone.

After quickly dressing, I hurried downstairs, past Mom and Dad, who was drinking their morning coffee, and outside to the garage. I couldn't believe what I saw: dozens of shiny marbles had been put back in the chest. When I finally turned around, Dad was standing there smiling.

He patted me on the head and said, Teddy's a good kid, I saw him too.

Soon, most of the marbles were returned to the wooden chest in our garage. Most of the kids in the neighborhood were good kids. I started playing again and began to share marbles with my friends. As often happens with kids (not often with adults) things began to even out. I eventually had only a normal supply of marbles in my jean pocket. Mom used the chest for something else, and the neighborhood was back to normal. I didn't need "all the marbles." Friends are more important than marbles. Buford was right once again.

It's the same on that yellow school bus bouncing along. There are mostly good, honest kids on the bus. Oh sure,

There are some bullies, some bad people, but mostly good kids just like you and me.

The chest full of beautiful marbles was real, and so were the events surrounding the chest. There are two large marbles sitting on my desk as I type this—all that remains of the treasure—more than 60 years later. You can read about the history of marble manufacturing in West Virginia.

As I remember those kids I knew so long ago, especially Teddy, I think of the final trip on that yellow school bus. The term will end, and there will be a final exam.

At the end of the term, it really will not matter who had the most marbles, or which school they went to, or who diagrammed all the sentences correctly.

There will probably be many disappointments at the end of the term for those who learned all the correct answers to questions they thought would be on the exam – questions about theory and acceptable practices.

The final exam doesn't have questions, just a checklist for those who pass:

☑ I was hungry, and you shared your lunch with me.

☑ I was thirsty, and you led me to the water fountain.

☑ I was new in town and you shared your marbles, so I could play.

☑ I didn't have good clothes, but you helped me find some.

☑ I was sick, and you took me to the nurse and stayed with me.

☑ I was in detention and you sat with me instead of going to recess.

After the marble story, every time I went to town, to see the big blind man, he would ask me, how many marbles do you have? I would then reach into my pocket and pull out a few marbles and put them in his big outstretched hand. Buford would smile as he touched each marble as though he could see them. Then he said, how many marbles do you want, Tim? Do you want all the marbles in town, or do you want just enough to play with the kids? That was a big lesson that I learned from Buford. Be content with having enough. Enough is all you need.

BUFORD AND HELEN KELLER AND FRIENDS

Choose your friends
and associates wisely.

Everyone makes mistakes.
Correct your mistakes,
and then learn from them.

L ooking back at those days, I'm amazed that my father never said anything to me about going downtown without permission. I think he sensed a big change in my attitude, attributable to my new friendship with the big blind man at the newspaper stand. To my father and I and everyone who knew the man, he was not a blind man, but Buford the smart, industrious, intelligent, and wise man who lived alone and provided for himself by running his little newspaper stand.

I didn't realize it then, but looking back from my current viewpoint, I'm sure that my father and Buford had a conversation about my visits downtown. And then too, that was many years ago when it was less dangerous for children to be on the streets. I cherish those simple days that made a lasting impression on my life. Most all the value that I now hold as an adult, I learned from my father and Buford.

For a long time after I met Buford, I wondered where he lived and how he did things without being able to see. I now realize that a human with determination can overcome handicaps and with the right attitude, be successful in life.

I had opened to the big man, and we had some good conversations, as well as possible between an older blind man and a young kid. In fact, we were becoming good friends. I asked him many questions, and he gave me lessons for life that remain with me even now.

The only thing I never really found out for sure was what had happened to his vision that was so bad that his eyes had to be removed. I do remember that it had to do with the war in Europe, World War I. I vaguely remember hearing Buford telling my father what had happened. It had something to do with nerve gas or poisoning. The sad thing was he lost his eyes in the service of our country.

I remember that Buford had graduated from an ivy league college in the east and had gone to a school for the blind to learn braille. There were so many things I want to learn about Buford.

Finally, curiosity about how he lived got the best of me.

I had never seen the big man anywhere other than at his newsstand. In the mind of a third grader, it appeared as if Buford had no home except the newsstand.

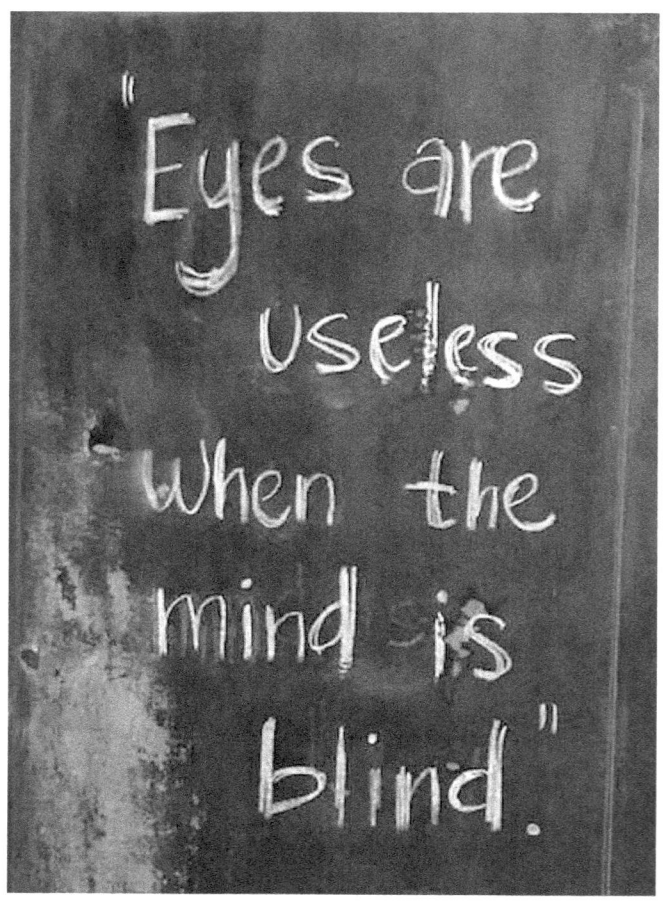

During one of my now, regular visits, I asked Buford, do you have a home? As was customary, the big man laughed as he threw back his big head and said, Tim, of course, I have a home, and I'm going to show it to you.

The big man hung up a sign which read, Out to lunch. We operate on the honor system. If you take something, please leave some money in the cup. Buford then picked up his white cane and said, come with me Tim we're going to see my house. Between the café and the hardware store next door, there was a single door, when opened, revealing a stairway which was private because it led to Buford's loft apartment over the café.

When we reached the top of the stairs, Buford said welcome to my home, Tim. It was dark inside Buford's apartment, and in my childhood innocence, I asked, how do you see in here Mr. Buford, it is so dark?

The big man then threw back his head, and with the biggest laugh, I've ever heard said, I don't need light to see Tim. That remains one of the most important lessons I learned from Buford. Seeing is an image in our mind. We receive that image not only through our vision but with all our other senses as well.

Buford turned on the single light in his apartment, which was a light bulb in the ceiling. I was amazed as I looked around because it looked so different than houses that I was used to. There were stacks of books and records. There was a single picture on the wall that I will never forget. Buford told me who the person in the picture was. With the most solemn voice I had ever heard, the big man told me the picture was of a very important woman, Helen Keller. Buford told me that he met Helen Keller when they were in college back East and for a time was deeply in love with her.

Buford told me that at one time he wanted to marry Miss Keller and he showed me a stack of letters from Miss Keller all written in braille. The big man said that Helen Keller at one time was the most important person in his life, and he still got an occasional letter from her. Buford seemed to have a tear in his heart, and a tremble on his lips when talking about Miss Keller.

There were only two things hanging on the wall of Buford's tiny home, a photograph of Helen Keller and his diploma from Harvard University.

Helen Keller had graduated from Radcliffe College in 1904. Buford, who was 10 years older than Helen was a brilliant young man from Coal Creek, West Virginia. At one time his parents were very wealthy from their interest in the coal mining industry and gave Buford the very best of educational opportunities. Buford had been awarded a scholarship to Harvard University but was unable to start his program because of the outbreak of the first World War.

Buford only served a few months of active duty in Europe before the incident that severely damaged his eyes. He remained in hospital in Europe for three months before returning to the United States. After six months of operations and treatments in American hospitals, Buford was finally headed east to Boston and on to Harvard University.

After enrolling at Harvard University, Buford continued to have problems with his eyes and eventually learned that he was going to become blind. His wealthy parents, fearing lawsuits from mining incidents that would deplete their fortune, quickly established a trust fund of a sizable amount to supply whatever Buford needed to finish his education at Harvard.

By this time Buford knew that he would be blind as his vision became more and more difficult. The trust fund that his parents set up paid for tutors and assistance to help him with anything he needed to do to finish university.

During his last couple of years at Harvard University, Buford was privileged to meet Helen Keller on several occasions. By this time, she had become very well known throughout the world and was writing books and being the spokesperson for many causes. She spoke several times at Harvard while Buford was there as a student.

Anne Sullivan, Helen's lifetime teacher, and assistant married a Harvard instructor, who was also one of Buford's teachers.

As a third grader at Pierpont Elementary school in Clarksville West Virginia, I did not remember all these things that Buford told me. But now as an adult, I can read the history books, and I'm astounded as I read about Helen Keller and her friends and associates, that all these things suddenly come back to me. It's thrilling to read history that I observed first hand by talking to Buford, my friend. The big, kind man obviously had been through many ups and downs in his lifetime and had suffered agonizingly the loss of his love not to death, but to her world popularity. I do remember Buford saying there was no other woman in his life after Helen Keller refused to marry him.

The amazing part of the story is from my earlier childhood. I was born in Florence, Alabama and we moved from there shortly thereafter. I began first grade at Pierpont school in Clarksville West Virginia. At the time when Buford was telling me about the stories, I did not realize that Helen Keller was born in Tuscumbia, Alabama just across the Tennessee River from Florence Alabama where I was born.

When Buford told me his history with Helen Keller, it seemed to be the one thing in all his life that he found regret in. It's hard to really understand—as a child—what an adult is trying to tell you, sometimes, but I believe Buford was trying to explain that we should never let anything stop us from living to the fullest that we possibly can. There will be disappointments and lost loves, lost bank accounts, lost friends lost homes and many other losses. But we must pick up the pieces and move forward. I often wondered why a man as intelligent as Buford worked every day of his life at a little newsstand in Clarksville, West Virginia. The question is answered in the asking. Even the smartest among us will make the wrong choices in life at some point. Thus we should always be willing to learn and despite all our difficulties, continue life's pathway—probably one of the greatest lessons that I learned from Buford, and he didn't realize I don't think, that he was teaching it to me. Or perhaps he did know. I will never know what happened in Buford's life; why a Harvard educated blind man was selling newspapers and magazines on the street in our little town in the hills of northern West Virginia.

Buford

As a kid, an elementary school kid, I had almost no concept of love, especially romantic love. My interest was in games, played with other boys. If I think about it, I can remember a little interest in girls. I begin to think about girls when my parents and I went to Canada with the Griffin family. Linda Griffin was older than me; and I liked her, even if she was a girl.

Tim, 8years old, with two native girls in North Bay, Ontario, Canada in 1949

I remember going to a birthday party of one of the girls in my class at Pierpont Elementary. The girl who was having the birthday insisted that we play spin-the-bottle. I was chagrined at the thought of kissing a girl, but I had to go along with the game. We all set in the circle on the floor. The first person spins a glass soda bottle, and when it stops, the girls it is pointing to is the girl you must kiss. Of course, if a girl spins the bottle, she must kiss a boy. My attitude about kissing a pretty girl has changed dramatically.

I now realize a lot of things I didn't understand when I was learning from Buford. I can now relate to him and the great pain he felt from rejection. Oh, I'm not without eyes like Buford, but they are growing dim. Over the 70 years since I knew Buford, I have inherited an incurable disease and being single again; I can understand the pain and anguish that my big friend must have felt. I can see now that the personal handicap was overshadowed by rejection. Even though Helen was blind—and more tragic, also deaf—she had become famous and had the support and help that Buford never had.

I have always remembered Buford as happy, laughing, and being pleasant. The only dark times were those moments when he was telling me about Helen.

I now understand his love and can feel his pain. Buford only wanted to love and to be loved, as do I.

Buford was not the only person, adult or child, that made an impression on me in the mountain town we lived in. My best friend was a little boy named Bernie Bryce, whose father managed the local grocery store where my father had a charge account. This caused me some amount of grief and a trip to the garage for corporal punishment, all because I could not resist the temptation to charge candy, on my father's account without permission. Bernie and I were almost constant companions having fun and getting in trouble like all little boys. One day while we were playing at his house, a repairman came to work on the washing machine in the basement of their home. Bernie and I could not resist watching the man work, and during his efforts to fix the washing machine he talked a lot to himself. At one point the repairman said I just couldn't get this old bitch to work right.

The reader of this story may already be ahead of me, and if so, it's because you understand little boys. A few days later I was working on my bicycle on the back porch of the preacher's home where we lived. The chain had come off my bicycle, and as I was trying to get it back on the bicycle, I said I just can't get this bitch back on. Well, that's what mothers are for—to keep an eye on young boys. I didn't realize that my mother was standing at the back door and heard every word I said. Intuitively, I knew I was in trouble because it was not a word that anyone used in my family. I wanted to get my punishment over with, but I had to wait

My Mother

until Dad got home that evening, of course, as soon as he got home, my mother told him what happened, and I was promptly invited for a visit to the garage where corporal punishment was administered as an aid to help me remember to be careful with my language.

I thought I was unjustly punished since I did not know what the word meant. So, the next afternoon after school I went to see my friend Buford. I told him the whole story and especially the part about not believing it to be fair. That's when Buford taught me one of the greatest lessons I've ever learned. He told me that the English language was one of the greatest blessings we could have. He also taught me that we should use the language carefully and with respect. Words have meaning. They can create peace or cause wars. And so, now as an old man, I still remember this lesson from Buford and try to use language with respect and decency. A person who continually uses foul language cannot be thought of as someone who appreciates one of the greatest blessings in life—our language.

Buford

My father, Clark David Harrison, was the pastor of the Central Christian Church in Clarksville and was well liked by members of his congregation and people throughout the community. My father was a tall, handsome man who was always dressed immaculately, even when playing his favorite game, croquet.

My father took the English game of croquet very seriously and was very good at the game. My father's croquet set was like the old Gospel big top. Those two items, along with my father's books, seemed to be our most important things

Buford once told me that you could understand a person by the things in life that are important to them. He always asked me how many marbles I had in my pocket.

I remember stories about many interesting people in my father's church. One of the most interesting people was a 90-year-old lady named Molly Robbins, who lived alone, drove her car, and was well known in Clarksville as the crazy woman driver. One Sunday morning Molly was on her way to church, and as usual, she was exceeding the speed limit.

A policeman on patrol stopped Molly and asked her where she was going in such a hurry. Molly looked up at the patrolman and said I'm going to church, you fool, where you ought to be. Without another word being spoken, Molly floor boarded it and sped away toward the church, leaving the police officer standing there with his mouth open.

One of my father's best friends at church, Paul McIntyre, went to great links to pull practical jokes. My father asked Paul's wife if she could find a photograph of him sitting down. She found an old picture when he was in the Navy, sitting on a pier. This was of course long before the Internet, Photoshop and things we take for granted today. My father took the picture and sent it to a professional artist, who hand-painted a picture of Paul sitting—not on a navy pier—but in an old wooden outhouse. Dad passed the picture around to Paul's friends, and they all had a good laugh about it. A few weeks later, Paul got his revenge. The pastor's house that we lived in was right behind the church, and in those days, we didn't always lock our doors. One Sunday we came home from church, and there was a lemon meringue pie, dad's favorite, sitting on the kitchen table. That was not unusual. People were always bringing food to the pastor's house, and if the door was unlocked, they would come in and set the food on the kitchen table.

When dad saw the fresh pie already sliced, he couldn't resist or wait, but quickly scooped up a precut piece of pie and took a large bite. It was just about the funniest thing I think I have ever seen.

Dad kept chewing on his bite of pie, and chewing, and chewing. By this time, it became obvious that the maker of the pie had done a tremendous job of making it look real, using cotton for the meringue part of the pie! For the next several days wherever dad went, people would ask him how his lemon meringue pie was. It seemed as if everyone in town knew, and they probably did after Paul McIntyre spread the story of the pastor and the fake pie.

When I saw Buford the next afternoon after school, he had already heard about dad and the lemon meringue pie. As usual, Buford saw a lesson for life in almost every situation, including the pie joke. He explained to me how important it is to have a sense of humor and to enjoy laughing. The big man told me that we should never take ourselves too seriously. Buford would throwback that big head of his and laugh so earnestly it was contagious. I can't remember a single time that I talked to Buford that he did not laugh during the conversation. That was quite amazing for a man who had no eyes. Even though Buford graduated from Harvard University and was very intelligent, he could have been indulging in self-pity. At times, Buford was sad like we all are. But he never let life's disappointments and failures define who he was or his life.

I never heard Buford complain about the many heartaches in his life. At one time his father was very wealthy. Buford's father owned several coal mining operations. But while Buford was in college there was a serious accident, a cave in at one of the Buford coal mines and several lives were lost. The ensuing investigations and trials left the family with almost nothing. But for the most part, the blind man accepted what had happened and was determined to make the most of life. And now, I remember Buford and his wonderful attitude toward life. I hope that I can always be like him.

A
NORMAN
ROCKWELL
THANKSGIVING

Buford

T hanksgiving with the Ab Wilson family, who were members of my father's church. The Wilsons lived on a big farm out in the country with a beautiful, large, two-story country home, barns with hay lofts to play in, a myriad assortment of animals and a wonderful family. The Wilsons had nine children.

Almost Heaven – West Virginia

When I learned that we were going to the Wilson farm for Thanksgiving Day,

I thought about my friend Buford, who had nowhere to go, and anyone to be with for Thanksgiving. I went into my father's study, a place you never went unless it was serious because he was always studying and preparing his sermons and it was not a good choice to interrupt him. I presented my case almost like a court drama. I pleaded with my father to let my friend Buford have Thanksgiving dinner with us. Being only eight years old, I probably shed a tear or two and got my father's undivided attention. In the end, I must've made a pretty good presentation, because my father agreed to invite Buford to go with us to the Wilson farm. Somehow my father knew that it would be all right with the Wilson family. They were loving, gracious, and caring people who accepted others with open arms.

I will always remember that day and have the picture firmly implanted in my mind of that large dining table with 15 people sitting quietly while Mr. Wilson told us about the importance of Thanksgiving. It was the scene right out of Currier and Ives, or Norman Rockwell. Mr. Wilson asked everyone to join hands and then said Mr. Burns would you please lead us in the prayer of Thanksgiving.

That Thanksgiving was very different and stands out in my mind as one of the best Thanksgivings I've ever had. After my dad drove downtown and we picked up Buford, we drove out to the beautiful countryside and the Wilson farm on the side of a mountain. We went early in the morning, because Thanksgiving, then was an all-day affair. After a scrumptious breakfast, the men and older boys left for the Turkey hunt on the mountain above the farm.

The younger kids played in the barnyard and in the hayloft. I asked my friend Buford to go for a walk with me, and I would show him the animals. I was beginning to think like Buford—that we can use our senses, other than eyesight, to create an image in our mind. I have never seen a person happier than Buford was that day. Not only did he feel accepted, he felt like he had a family. As we walked around the big barnyard, the big man would describe for me what he was seeing. The visions he had in his mind aided by the sounds and smells of the barnyard were as real to him as the visual image was to me.

Looking back, I believe it was one of the best days that Buford and I ever had together. I will not forget the lesson learned, that images are in our mind, and they are just as real to the blind person as they are to the seeing person. Whatever our handicap in life is, we can compensate if we try hard enough. The sad thing is, there are so many who give up and never try.

It was a glorious autumn morning, and before long we heard gunshots up on the mountain, and Buford threw back that enormous head and laughed and laughed. He squeezed my hand tight and said Tim; we are going to have turkey for Thanksgiving. It was quite a sight to see the men and older boys coming down off the mountain top holding several turkeys, with broad smiles on their faces. It was truly an old-fashioned Thanksgiving.

As my father began to pray, Buford squeezed my hand, and I could feel him trembling slightly, trembling, I now believe out of joy and gratitude. I believe it was one of the most important days of the big man's life. I can't begin to express how important the human touch is, in the friendship of love. Every Thanksgiving I think of that big table and good honest people sitting around it, enjoying the bounty of the harvest and enjoying one another.

That Thanksgiving with the Wilson family, my father, and mother, and my friend and mentor, Buford, was the Thanksgiving I will always remember. It was a scene that can only be painted by Norman Rockwell or Currier and Ives. Thanksgiving is the best of American tradition.

THE HORSE WHISPERER

Respect all life,
human and animals.

Always be
kind.

Be gentle with all
people and animals

Buford

One of my favorite memories of growing up in Clarksville was the day Buford became a horse whisperer, a person with the uncanny, almost supernatural power to calm and control animals.

My father had become friends with Mr. Nathan Goff, a wealthy and successful businessman who owned an estate in the beautiful rolling countryside just beyond the city limits of Clarksville I don't remember what Mr. Goff did, career-wise, but I will never forget his passion for Clydesdale horses. There is a building in Clarksville called the Goff Building.

Long before the popular television commercials of Budweiser, picturing the elegant, stately and beautiful Clydesdale horses, Mr. Goff owned a stable full of genuine Clydesdales. The horses were not used for anything other than the pleasure of the owner.

Mr. Goff's Clydesdales

Looking back to those days and remembering the many times I saw Mr. Goff and his team of Clydesdales pulling a red wagon. I'm filled with nostalgia, remembering those beautiful creatures.

The vision in my memory is of a foggy morning with the beautiful mountains of autumn in the background, and Mr. Goff holds the reins of a beautiful team of horses. It was a scene I saw quite frequently. Every Saturday morning without fail except for poor weather, Mr. Goff would have his workers prepare the Clydesdale horses and harness them to a shiny wagon. Mr. Goff and invited guests would tour the estate riding high on the seat of the red wagon behind those magnificent creatures.

As I remember, my father experienced that ride several times, but the most memorable time was the Saturday morning they took me along, with Mr. Goff's approval, to ride behind the Clydesdales. No carnival ride, airplane ride or any other type of ride has thrilled me as much is that Saturday morning riding behind the Clydesdales.

That experience was limited to only a few of Mr. Goff's special friends, as only two people other than the wagon master could ride in the high seat.

I don't know a lot about the temperament of Clydesdale horses, but I do know they are magnificent creatures and when they are young and full of life they must be broken. I prefer the word trained. Mr. Goff explained that his horses matured and became old and had to be replaced by younger horses to maintain a good dependable team. Like the young of many species, young Clydesdale horses can be adventuresome.

Misty Morning and Clydesdales

It was in the spring, early spring when the buds were just starting to pop out in the trees, the time when the males of all species become restless. A young Clydesdale horse recently added to Mr. Goff's stable broke through the stable gates early one day, perhaps an hour before sunrise.

The young, exuberant Clydesdale began running across the countryside. The Goff farm was perhaps five miles from the heart of town. Just as the sun cleared the horizon signaling the start of a new work day, the young horse galloped into the city limits of Clarksville. It would be an understatement to tell you the strong young horse caused pandemonium in downtown Clarksville, West Virginia on that morning.

The young, strong horse got into several altercations with automobiles and kicked in their doors, as well as glass and some storefronts. Panic set-in over the whole city; the young horse seemed to be enjoying his freedom and was celebrated by causing as much mischief as it could. The rampage went on for a few hours until the horse turned down the street where the café was, next door to Buford's newsstand.

Then an amazing thing happened. The horse suddenly stopped and stood perfectly still in front of Buford. The blind man held out his hand, palm down in front of him and stood very still and quiet. While the horse sniffed of his hand, Buford talked quietly to the horse. By this time a few hundred people had gathered close to Buford's newsstand to observe the amazing spectacle. As Buford continued to talk quietly to the horse, he finally reached for the horse's neck and started petting him.

Buford quietly said will someone please go next door to the hardware store and get some rope. Buford took the rope and gently put it over the horse's head and around his neck and held him still. Everyone who was a witness to the amazing events of that day would tell you the horse became as gentle as a small puppy when Buford was talking to it.

The image of a huge, exuberant Clydesdale horse standing in front of Buford, the big blind man covered the front page of the *Clarksville Times* the next morning. The photograph and story were picked up by national news organizations, and so on Buford and the Clydesdale were celebrities all over the country. This all occurred many decades before the term horse whisperer was coined and a book and a movie were produced on the subject.

I was so impatient for the time to pass until I can go downtown the next day and see my hero, Buford, who had become an overnight celebrity as a man who could hypnotize animals.

It seemed Buford could read my mind. When I approached his newsstand the next day, he threw back his head and laughed and said, Tim, what do you want my autograph?   I replied, Mr. Buford you are the most famous person in the world. Being the humble man that he was, Buford laughed harder than I ever heard him laugh.

And that started another session of valuable lessons for life that I learned from Buford. He said, Tim, let's talk a while. He then said that the important thing in life is to be a real person, not a fake or a hypocrite or show off. Never think that you are better than you are and never be arrogant, but always humble and kind. When you do something well in life, enjoy your success. But never let it change who you are. If Buford were around today, he would probably say enjoy your 15 minutes of fame, but don't let it change your character.

I listened to Buford because if I didn't Buford would quit telling me things. I heard him say many times that you shouldn't waste your time trying to teach someone who is unwilling to learn. Only after listening carefully, would Buford let me ask questions. That day I had only one question for Buford. What kind of magic did he have to control that huge Clydesdale horse? When I asked, I knew there would be two valuable lessons for the day or at least more than one.

Buford began the second lesson by saying, Tim, all life is sacred and important. Nations have not learned that lesson yet, and that's why we have wars. Most people think that animals are not as smart as we are, but in some ways, they are smarter than we are. People have brains and intelligence; animals have instinct. Their instinct helps them survive. That's the reason wild animals run from humans; instinct tells them they could be in danger.

Buford always knew my questions before I asked them. He said Tim; I know you were wondering why the horse did not run from me. Animals can sense good people, and they can sense bad people. I don't know how they do it, but I've learned that if you are a kind and gentle person with an animal and show it respect you can win its confidence. First, you should never be aggressive. Gently hold out your hand palm down and give the animal a chance to smell. Humans give off different odors to different situations. Animals can smell fear and friendliness.

Well, the lesson went on for quite a while. I could tell that Buford loved animals. Looking back over my lifetime and then reading a book and seeing a movie about horse whisperers, I realize that Buford had all the characteristics of a true horse whisperer, a person that animals trust and are willing to be trained by that person.

I have never forgotten that valuable lesson and every time I see a dog, they show me the same respect that the horse showed Buford. I never reach for a dog, but simply hold my hand out toward the dog, bottom-up (showing your hand bottom up means you are not aggressive) and give the dog long as it wants to smell my intentions. I give the dog long enough to become satisfied that I'm a good person, then I can then pet them all day long. I have won their confidence just like Buford won the confidence of that young

Clydesdale horse in 1949 in the mountains of West Virginia.

Looking back now, I realize that one of the most valuable lessons I ever learned from Buford, was one that was not talked about specifically, but it ran concurrently with all the other lessons. And that is the lesson of being patient. All good things in life take time to develop – and not only time but determination and dedication to those things that are important. Buford was patient with a Clydesdale horse, just as he was patient with a little elementary school boy who was fascinated by the big blind man. My relationship with Buford took time to develop to the point where we trusted one another and looked forward to being with each other. Oh, I really didn't realize those things then, but they were lessons which would stay with me the rest of my life. It's probably one of the greatest lessons Buford ever taught me, not verbally, but by example. It takes time, dedication and determination to make a great friendship. A lasting friendship does not occur overnight, but as the preparation of good food, it takes time.

We never learn the great lessons of life from a single individual, but from our parents, teachers, friends and occasionally, a wonderful person like Buford who we find unexpectedly.

There are many things I do not know about Buford, after all, I was just a boy in elementary school, who loved to play marbles and all the other games that kids play. We went to school, not simply because we wanted to, but because it's a part of living in a civilized society. The elders teach the young. But it's the things that come along in our lives by serendipity that make the difference. Buford, Ms. De Vita, and the friends of my parents, all made a lasting impression on my life.

The amazing thing is that some of the best lessons in life that we were taught when we were young are not remembered until we become old. That's one of the tragedies of life, that each generation makes its own mistakes, repeating the same mistakes of past generations, repeatedly. If only we would listen to the wisdom of those who have been on the journey, who knows what we will face, then each generation would become better, but that does not happen, sadly.

THE
COAL MINE
EXPLOSION

All life is important.

Human life is sacred.

Altruistic love is the
the most-convincing
argument for a
Creator.

Buford

I n northern West Virginia, coal mining is part of the culture and history; and is a vital part of the economy.

Probably the closest friends my parents had during those years were the Griffins. The Griffins lived on a beautiful estate out in the countryside from Clarksville. Mr. Clark Griffin owned a large coal mining operation. He was probably one of the largest operators of coal mining during the time we lived in West Virginia. We went to the Griffin home frequently to visit, dine and watch movies.

This was in the 1940s, and we didn't have television, but Mr. Griffin owned his own movie projector, and every time we went to their home, we watched movies. You may not remember the <u>Three Stooges</u>, but Mr. Griffin had every <u>Three Stooges</u> movie ever made, and we watched them over and over.

Mr. Griffin was a great outdoorsman who loved hunting and fishing, as did my father. That is probably the bond that formed their friendship. I remember that my father went hunting in the snow-covered forest of West Virginia, for black bears and white-tailed deer. Mr. Griffin and my father obviously had a common love of the outdoors, and in 1949 we were invited to go to Canada on a fishing trip with the Griffin family. The Griffins had one daughter, Linda, who was two or three years older than me. I was eight years old, but I remember almost every detail of that trip to Canada. In fact, I had my eighth birthday during that trip to Canada. Many years later, my daughter would have her eighth birthday on a remote island deep in the Canadian wilderness of Ontario, Canada.

We went to North Bay, Ontario to Lake Nipissing. Mr. Griffin and my father fished for Northern Pike, and we stayed in tiny cabins with ice boxes. There was no electricity, no refrigerators, but every day a truck would come and bring ice which had been cut out of the lake during the winter and stored in stacks covered with sawdust, to last all summer.

Of all the trips and vacations during my lifetime, that trip with the Griffin family to North Bay, Ontario, is as vivid as if it happened yesterday.

I have vivid memories of the hard-working coal miners in the mining industry of West Virginia. To this day, I believe that being a coal miner is one of the most difficult jobs a man can have. While we were living in the mountain state, one of the largest coal mines had a cave-in, trapping several men far underground.

The cave-in became an all-consuming event for people in northern West Virginia, especially those in Clarksville where we lived. All coal mining ceased, and a great effort made to find and free the trapped miners; for many days that was the only subject of conversation and activity in Clarksville.

The entrance of the mine that caved in was becoming a small town or community, with activity 24 hours a day in the recovery effort. It became critical, after several days, because if the men were still alive, they had no food or water and probably a limited amount of oxygen.

After several days of the recovery effort, the team believed they were close to finding the men. But the dilemma facing the recovery team was choosing the right direction to go, as there were different tunnels leading off from the caved-in area. Finally, it was determined that there was too little time to try to drill into three different tunnels, and a decision had to be made which was the most likely tunnel that led to the men who were trapped.

The best audio equipment available at that time was brought into the mine to determine if the men were alive and if so, which tunnel they were in. Time was critical, and it was finally determined that they needed someone with extra sensitive hearing to monitor the equipment. This was the only thing people were talking about in Clarksville West Virginia during those disastrous days. My father took an increasingly close interest in the development because of his friend Clark Griffin, who had an interest in that mine.

When I came home from school that evening, dad was explaining all this to my mother, and I listened intently. Finally, I told my father that Buford had the best hearing of anyone. I said, Dad, Buford can hear anything, that's how he sees things. My father was never one to speak quickly but always thought several moments before answering. That was a result of his childhood when the teacher told him to always think three times before speaking. Finally, Dad said Timothy; I think you are right. They need

Buford to listen to that equipment because of his sensitive hearing.

Time was running short, so Dad knew he had to decide in a hurry. Because I was now Buford's best friend, Dad let me come along. We went downtown, and Dad explained the dire situation to Buford, who of course already knew everything about the cave-in. After all, Buford ran a newsstand. He knew everything that was happening.

The big man never hesitated a moment and said, Reverend, if you will help me close the newsstand, I'll be ready to go. Within a few minutes my dad and I, and Buford were headed out of town and driving swiftly to the coal mine. When we arrived, I was totally in awe of the small city that had sprung up in the middle of nowhere with men and equipment involved in the rescue effort. When I saw the magnitude of the recovery site, I knew that it was a big deal. I was so proud that Buford was going to become a part of the rescue effort.

Dad quickly started asking people directions to find the director of rescue operations, which took time because of all the confusion. Finally, we found the man in charge, and Dad introduced him to Buford saying this man has the most sensitive hearing of any person we have ever known. He is willing to help in the operations.

The head of the recovery team was reluctant at first. He thought it was risky taking a blind man down into the coal mine, but he knew time was short and they must do everything possible to rescue the men. He explained to Buford that he might be down there possibly 24 hours, that it was cold and uncomfortable and dark down deep in the mind where the rescue was taking place. Buford, being the humanitarian that he was, never hesitated a moment, but said he would do anything possible to save a life.

Buford knew the chance he was taking and took time to shake my dad's hand and bent over and told me, don't worry my little friend, I will be okay. I've got to do this. They gave Buford a backpack with blankets, water, and food and I watched him as he was loaded into the transport which soon disappeared into the darkness of the mine. Dad gave his telephone number to the director of the recovery and said we couldn't stay out here all night, but if you call me, I will come as quickly as I can. Dad then said I would be back in the morning. The way dad said it, I knew that I would have to go to school.

Another great lesson learned from Buford, perhaps the most important, is the altruistic component of the human makeup. I now realize that the altruistic nature that allows men and women to risk and even sacrifice their own lives to save someone else is one of the strongest arguments for divine creation. Darwinism says that choices and development favor the strongest and it is this aspect which is the major thesis of Darwinian evolution. Buford went down deep within the earth at great risk to his own life because there were humans down there and he felt a compelling urge to do what he could to help save their lives, even at the risk of losing his own life. Life is better lived with fellow humans. The happiest people are those who have companionship and friends with other people. Often, we take those we love for granted, but I learned from Buford and from my own experience how important it is to love someone, and care deeply for them; even sacrificing my life for those, I love.

My friend Buford spent almost 24 hours in that dark, cold and gloomy world deep within the earth. He listened intently to the sounds collected by the audio equipment that had been sent to the rescue site.

His efforts did contribute to the selection of the correct tunnel that the five coal miners were trapped in. Once the tunnel was selected, the rescue workers worked feverishly clearing debris that was blocking the tunnel. The five miners were found still alive but in critical condition. They were quickly transported to the surface and to hospitals for treatment. They all survived.

The pride that I felt for my friend, Buford, for helping to rescue the trapped miners, far surpassed the pride I felt when he helped calm the Clydesdale horse. It should not come as a surprise, that the value of human life is sacred and is a shadow of the divine. The lessons I learned from Buford and the lessons I have learned since have led me to believe that everyone has a story to tell and every story is important. There are no unimportant people. There are those who have gone astray, committed crimes and atrocities against mankind. But in the beginning, in their infancy, they began life as innocent infants.

MY
BIG BROTHER

You have two choices. You can let your mistakes destroy you, or you can learn from them and become a better person.

My brother, John Claude Harrison, was 10 years older than me. I looked up to him, just as I did Buford, the man with no eyes. In some respects, I was closer to Buford, because my brother was away in a boarding school for much of my youth. Buford was sensitive to relationships and never failed to ask me how my big brother was doing.

After my brother graduated from a Christian high school in Athens, Alabama, he came home to the hills of West Virginia for the Summer.

My father had a daily radio program on the local radio station WPD X. In the Summer, when he was home from school, my brother who was only 19 years old, spoke on my father's radio program.

My brother was a natural trader and, in the summers, when he was home from boarding school, he learned to become a pilot and had his own airplane. I remember that it was red and yellow.

My father had decided to send my brother to the college he had graduated

from, Garrett, Christian college, in
Henderson, Tennessee.

So, by the end of that summer, John
Claude had managed to not only have his
own airplane but a Harley-Davidson
motorcycle in addition. In preparation for
his first year of college down in
Tennessee, John Claude traded his

interests in the airplane and the motorcycle for an antique, long bed truck, that he and his friend, Lawrence Taylor, drove to Henderson Tennessee that fall, where they both became a freshman at Garrett Christian college.

I remember one special Sunday that summer John Claude was home. Most of the Sundays and weekends, he was preaching at small churches in the northern mountain communities of West Virginia. I will never forget the weekend that my big brother took me with him on one of his preaching assignments. The community was called Pumpkin Center, West Virginia. Pumpkin Center was a small coal mining community, but it did have a movie theater, something I had never been to before.

After making me promise not to tell my parents, my brother took me to the first movie I had ever seen in a real theater. It's been almost 70 years now, but I remember the movie. It was an old, science fiction-type movie.

Keeping my word to my big brother, I never told my parents that we went to a movie that weekend. Later I told my friend, Buford, about the weekend with my brother. Buford sensed that I was conflicted about not telling my parents.

Buford said, let's set down for a while and let me explain something to you. Buford explained something that I have never forgotten. It was a rule of personal moral conduct. He said you did nothing wrong by going to the movie with your brother. Perhaps your brother made a mistake by making you promise not to tell.

Buford said, Tim, as you get older, you will realize there are things in our personal lives that we don't need to share with everyone.

If your parents had asked you, did you go to a movie and you said no, that would be a lie. Or if your parents had told you to never go to a movie without telling them, then that would be deceptive.

Buford gently explained, that my big brother did not use good judgment when he told me not to tell. I didn't understand everything that Buford was saying, but I remember his words. He explained that my brother put me in a position of moral conflict. That is something that everyone faces during their lifetime. We each have personal decisions to make, and those decisions become the foundation stones in developing our character.

In one of the greatest lessons that Buford ever taught me, he explained that we make many mistakes in life and we have two choices. We can let the mistakes destroy us, or we can learn from our mistakes and become better people.

Buford explained that the choices we make are not always good, and we each make mistakes, but if we have the right attitude, each mistake is an opportunity to grow.

I honestly don't remember if my parents ever knew that my big brother took me to my first movie, but I will never forget that weekend with my brother and the lesson from Buford.

Our Parents

Buford

A STAR
IS BORN

Buford becomes the hero of a city.

Do not let pride destroy you. Remember, there is always someone greater and someone lesser than yourself.

Never quit learning

After the coal mine explosion and Buford's successful efforts in the rescue operation, he became well-known throughout the Northern part of West Virginia, and the fame and attention were well deserved, even though at times I was sure I had lost my friend and hero to fame deserving of a true hero.

After the publicity in newspapers throughout the United States, it was inevitable that Buford would receive the attention he so greatly deserved.

The trust fund that Buford's parents had established when it became known that one day, he would be totally blind, along with the meager earnings from his newsstand had sustained him through the years.

Clarksville was a prosperous city of thirty thousand people, and Buford was probably the most well know and liked citizen in this beautiful mountain city.

Job offers and opportunities started pouring in for the man with no eyes. Finally, the owner of Robert's Hardware next door to the City Café, recognizing an opportunity, hired Buford to work in the only hardware store in Clarksville.

Many years before Walmart stores and their "greeters," Bufford was hired as a greeter at Robert's Hardware. Buford had his own desk just inside the front door, and that desk became one of the most popular places in the city. People would often wait in line to meet Buford, the horse whisperer and hero of the coal mine explosion.

I was proud of my friend, Buford, but also a little jealous of his friendship. I had come to think of the big man as my friend. But now, Buford was the hero of a city and people wanted to meet him.

Buford became an advisor and was asked dozens of questions and personal advice almost every day. Buford certainly brought business into the hardware store.

The amazing part of the story, Buford, the big man with no eyes, never let his celebrity change him. Every time I went to the hardware store after school, Buford was happy to see me, and he even kept a special chair next to his at the desk for me.

I was certainly proud of the honor of having my own chair next to Buford. The kids at Pierpont Elementary were certainly impressed, but Buford kept a close watch on me and kept me from becoming conceited. He could always tell when "I was becoming too big for my britches," and would invite me to have a "special talk."

In one of his greatest lessons, Buford taught me the foolishness of pride. He explained that there is always someone lesser and someone greater than yourself. Only compare yourself today with yourself of yesterday. Your only concern should be with becoming the best person you can be.

Buford never let his successes and accomplishments change him. He remained the kind and gentle man he had always been. The only thing different was the honor which he had earned, was becoming known.

Buford took every opportunity to explain to me the value of personal diligence to education and learning every day. The fact that Buford had graduated from one of the most famous universities in the world was not as important to him as learning every day.

I didn't realize it then of course, but Buford always asked me many questions. I now know the two reasons Buford would use to explain. First, Buford would say, "Everyone has a story to tell, and every story is important."

The second reason, Buford would explain, is that the wise man will continue to learn until his last day on earth.

I didn't understand all these things, then of course, but I remember them. And now Buford's sayings and understanding about life have become my own.

LEAVING CLARKSVILLE AND BUFORD

Buford

L ife is filled with disappointments and change is inevitable, if anything at all. One of the greatest causes of stress in my childhood was the many times we moved when I was growing up. I didn't understand then, and I still don't, why we moved so many times when I was young.

My father was well liked and respected by people throughout the United States. Now, that I am older than my father was when he died, I still hear from people across the country who praise him for being a positive influence in their lives.

But, much to my sadness, we moved every three or so years until I was in high school.

When my father and mother told me, we were moving to Flint, Michigan;

my world came crashing down. When It finally became clear to me what that decision entailed, I asked my father, "But what about Buford?"

I realize that it may seem strange that a 10-year-old kid can become that attached to a big man with no eyes, but then most people have never met a man like Buford.

For several days I was angry at my parents about leaving Clarksville and Buford and moving to a strange place.

Finally, my father promised me that in the summers we would come back to see Buford. As kids always do, I finally accepted the decision I did not understand.

I don't remember telling Buford goodbye, but I do remember a crumpled piece of paper that Buford gave me with his name and address. I wish I could tell you about our parting words, but having studied the behavioral sciences, I know we tend to put unpleasant things out of our memory.

But I would never forget Buford.

Buford's story and our friendship do not end here.

Buford

MICHIGAN AND A NEW HERO

Don't be afraid to go into your library and read every book.

The supreme quality for leadership is unquestionably integrity.

-Dwight David Eisenhower

I t was a cold night in 1952, and the excitement was growing. I was 11, and it was past midnight, the first time I had been permitted to stay up all night.

Dad and I had a big bowl of popcorn and were intent on the voices in the beautiful old Zenith console radio. My hero, 5-Star General, Dwight David Eisenhauer was in the lead of the presidential voting returns, and it looked like he was to become the President of the United States!

He was a hero of the free world. Eisenhower, Roosevelt and England's Churchill had been the leaders in saving the world from Hitler's efforts to dominate the world. For the time being, Buford and his world were forgotten.

I had traded Pierpont, a school in Clarksville, W. VA. for Walker school in Flint, Michigan.

That Summer we went to downtown Flint to the Eisenhower campaign headquarters to see how many "I Like Ike" campaign buttons we could fill our pockets with. All the kids "liked Ike."

Eisenhower had become my hero that autumn and after all the years, one of the most exciting moments of my life. Ike was coming to Flint that autumn for a campaign speech and I wanted more than anything to see him in person. But my mother would not let me skip school that day Eisenhower was in town.

The day of the speech came, and I went trudging off the Walker Elementary School. It was to become one of the most exciting days of my life. Walker School took up an entire city block. It was only a few blocks from the heart of the city. The boys in the 6th grade had the opportunity to become patrolmen and assist the other kids crossing the streets at the intersections surrounding the school.

It was a great honor to be selected as a patrolman and along with the responsibility went an official badge and a web belt/shoulder belt to which the badge was attached.

Several of the grade-school kids went home for lunch. Thus the patrolmen had to be on duty at your assigned street corner.

I was on my assigned corner as lunch was almost over and there were four or five other kids at my corner. Suddenly, we heard sirens and looking up we saw several motorcycle cops and several long limos slowly approaching our corner. One of the long, black limos was a convertible, and as it approached our corner, it slowed almost to a complete stop and a regal-looking man stood up from the rear seat and at the moment the limo was in the intersection of my corner, one of the most important men in the world, one of only a hand-full of 5-star generals of the United States, saluted me and a hand-full of kids on a street corner in Flint Michigan. The General was a great man!

I suddenly remembered the crumpled piece of paper on which Buford had written his address. The paper was now in my father's lockable chest of important papers.

That evening I had a grand story to tell as we ate dinner together; I also had an important letter to write – with the help of my mother—to my friend Buford in Clarksville, West Virginia. I had to tell

Buford about the General who saluted me, the General who was soon to become the President of the United States of America.

I wrote a letter, with my mother's help, to the big blind man in the Northern mountains of West Virginia. I was proud of the man Buford had become and wanted to share with him my adventures in my newly adopted home state, Michigan.

A few weeks later, I was thrilled when I came home from school, and my mother had a surprise waiting for me. It was a treasure, a letter from Buford. Included in the letter was a photo of the window façade of Robert's hardware. There was a new sign painted on the front plate-glass window of Roberts' Hardware:

Roberts' Hardware

Clarksville, W.VA.

Home of

Buford,

Horse Whisperer

Philosopher

Advisor

Hero

As I looked at the photograph, my mother read Buford's letter to my father and me. When she came to the part where he gave me credit for having faith in him and was the reason for his success, the tears started flowing freely from all three of us, Mom, Dad and myself.

Well, there is one thing I knew for sure, and it was this: There are good people left in this world, and there is none better than Buford, the man with no eyes.

All three of us treasured the letter and photograph from Buford, and we placed them in Dad's small, portable safe where important family treasures were kept.

The photograph of the sign on the window in front of Robert's Hardware told the whole story. It was a lesson that has stayed with me through life. The lessons of Buford and my new hero, General Dwight David Eisenhower, boiled down to respect, honor, integrity and the "golden rule" of life, found in some form in all the major religions and honorable organizations in the world,

Treat people the way you want to be treated,

Or

Do unto others as you would have them do unto you.

T Time is the equalizer of all things, and to time we each must pay homage, for when our "three scores and ten" are up and there is no more sand in our upper globe of opportunity, then time for each of us comes to an end.

In Michigan, time moved swiftly, for I was at the age when boys are full are dreams, dreams of being a major league baseball pitcher for the Detroit Tigers or an explorer, photographing the great herds of animals on the endless plains of Africa.

Before I hardly had time to move out of adolescence, it was time to start thinking about college.

During junior high school and high school years, my great friend Buford had kept up with my progress, always concerned that I make the right decisions.

Buford was concerned about my choice of colleges, even offering to help me apply to his alma mater, Harvard University. But Harvard was out of my reach financially, if not academically. Buford and his kindness and love for me assured me that I had the intellect, if not the funds, for a Harvard education.

There was a small college in the northern mountains of West Virginia that had great appeal to my father and me, at least for the undergraduate years. It was a private college associated with the Christian churches/churches of Christ, Bethany College in the beautiful mountain town of Bethany West Virginia.

Even though I was only a teenager, I realized that some of the greatest lessons I had learned in life so far came from my friend Buford, the man with no eyes.

I wrote a long letter to Buford asking his advice about Bethany College in Bethany West Virginia as a school to do my undergraduate work in. Realizing that it was only a 2-hour drive from Clarksville to Bethany, Buford seemed excited about the idea.

I did not know it at the time, but I had become something of a minor celebrity in Clarksville West Virginia, because of my friendship with Buford, the man with no eyes.

I mentioned earlier that Buford kept a small chair beside his desk for me when I came to visit. It even had a hand-lettered sign which reads," Timothy's chair." Of course, everyone who came into the hardware store and spoke to Buford would ask about the chair. Buford always replied that chair belongs to my best friend, Timothy Dwight Harrison.

That was another great lesson from Buford, that true friendship is based on love and respect, and has nothing to do with age or position in life.

It wasn't until the college years that I realized the meaning of true friendship.

When I returned as a college freshman to the mountains of West Virginia and saw that chair beside Buford's desk, I realized then that friendship goes both ways. I never thought of myself doing anything for Buford, but he reminded me that I was the only one who had confidence in him when I was just a child in elementary school.

THE COLLEGE YEARS

Not by years, but by disposition, is wisdom acquired.

In 1960 I drove my 1955 Chevrolet to Bethany, West Virginia to begin my college years at Bethany College, a private college founded by Alexander Campbell.

Originally settled in 1769, Bethany West Virginia had previously been inhabited by the Mingo and Shawnee nations.

The town of Bethany was given its name by the founder of Bethany College, Alexander Campbell, in 1827

The American frontier of the early 19th century was brimming with religious fervor. While the human spirit was being awakened in the cities of the United States, there was a special intensity to the revivals of the frontier. My father had been a student of the history of the

Restoration Movement and we had visited Bethany many times when we lived in Clarksville. He was very happy that I had chosen Bethany College, where I enrolled as a freshman in Psychology and Ministry.

Of course, I didn't go directly to Bethany but drove straight to Clarksville and Robert's Hardware.

It was a joyful reunion. Buford reached out for my shoulders, to judge how tall I had grown. Tear's came to my eyes when I saw the chair—the one with my name on it beside Buford's desk.

Word quickly spread that Buford's friend, Timothy Dwight Harrison was back in town and soon Robert's Hardware was filled with people listening to the old stories when I was just a kid.

He retold the story of the Clydesdale horse and the coal mine explosion.

Buford and I went next door to lunch at the old City Café and had a root beer float. The old flower box under the front window was still there, filled with flowers.

Buford, jokingly, asked me to close my eyes and tell him what I heard.

It was the perfect homecoming of an old blind man and his young friend.

THE
GIFT

Buford

When choosing Bethany college, I honestly thought that I would go to Clarksville and see Buford every Saturday. I didn't know then, that being a freshman in college could demand so much time.

There were football games, of course, parties, and naturally, pretty girls. Speaking of pretty girls, that was the subject of one of my early visits that year to Buford.

During our many conversations when I was growing up in Clarksville, I knew about Buford and his love affair with the famous Helen Keller. But it was a subject that Buford and I seldom mentioned, either because of his reluctance or my young age, at which I had little interest in girls.

Ivy Green, Tuscumbia, Alabama, birth home of Hellen Keller.

But when I returned to West Virginia as a college freshman my interest in, and attitude toward girls had taken on a new perspective.

Buford, in his wisdom and understanding of the human nature, realized all this intuitively. As a result, our visits together and his lessons of life for me began to center more and more on romantic relationships. Buford began to tell me more about his friendship with Helen Keller. It became obvious as I listened that the relationship with Helen Keller was one of the great disappointments of his life.

Remembering the past discussions with Buford about Helen Keller, I became quite interested in this phenomenal person and did a couple of book reports in high school about Helen Keller. I told Buford about my studies of Helen Keller and her life and reminded Buford that we were born on opposite sides of the Tennessee River. I was born on the Northside of the river, in a beautiful, Renaissance City, Florence Alabama. Helen Keller was born just south of the Tennessee River in a city called Tuscumbia. Our birthplaces were no more than 10 or 12 miles apart.

This conversation about Helen Keller seemed to affect my friend more than anything we had ever talked about. It was almost as if I had become the teacher and Buford the pupil. The home that Helen grew up in is now a protected treasure called Ivy Green, Buford was very quiet and attentive to every word I said.

Almost every trip I made that fall to Clarksville, the subject of our conversations usually came around to Helen Keller.

By December, I had come up with the idea of taking a trip with Buford to visit Ivy Green. I talked to my father, and he agreed to my proposal of taking a train trip with Buford to Tuscumbia Alabama.

Just before our Christmas recess, I went to see Buford and told him I had a special Christmas present for him. I then handed him the two train tickets. He held them a long time, turning them over and over. It was almost as if he could read the ink on the paper by feel. He did know somehow; they were something extremely important.

When I asked Buford how long it has been since he had taken a trip, he began to tremble, and big tears rolled down his cheeks. I said, Buford, they are two train tickets for March, during our Spring Break.

Buford and I had become such good friends; it was almost as if we could read each other's mind. He simply said, Ivy Green? I didn't have to answer, he already knew.

I then told Buford, that my father had written a letter to the agency responsible for Ivy green and told them about our trip. I explained that he would be given special permission to touch everything at Ivy green, the beautifully preserved childhood home of Helen Keller under the soothing canopy of the old stately trees.

The only way I can describe Buford's reaction is to tell you that he was stunned, and I knew it was one of the happiest moments of his life. By this time

30 or 40 people had gathered around Buford's desk at the hardware store. After a few moments, the original shock had worn off replaced by one of the biggest smiles I have ever seen Buford had become such a celebrity in Clarksville that a group of people was always available to hear Buford stories.

That day—when I handed Buford the train tickets—will never be forgotten. That's the day that I learned about unselfish giving and the reciprocal gratitude of receiving. I learned the truth of the ancient adage that it truly is

More blessed to give, than to receive.

Many people would ask why I would take a blind man on a 1500-mile train trip to see a home. I would respond, with Buford's greatest lesson of all:

There are more ways of
seeing, then only with
the eyes.

THE

TRAIN

ADVENTURE

From West Virginia to Ivy Green, Tuscumbia, Alabama

Buford

T he train was slowing down, and I knew we were approaching Clarksville West Virginia where I was going to pick up my friend Buford for our special trip to Ivy Green, the birthplace of Helen Keller, in Tuscumbia, Alabama.

When the conductor announced our arrival in Clarksville, I looked out the window, and there was Buford, standing tall and proud in a brand-new suit with tie and beautiful hat.

I was amazed and totally unprepared for what I saw, dozens and dozens of people gathered around Buford, who had come to see him off on his much-anticipated journey. There was a man that looked like an old soldier from World War I with a trumpet, and children with balloons.

There was a large hand-lettered sign, wishing Buford well on his trip

When the train finally came to a complete stop, I rushed down the stairs to see my friend. He placed his hands on my shoulders and said, Timothy Dwight Harrison, we have come a long way together. I said Buford, please don't say any more right now. We have all night to talk on the train. Buford smiled and said Timothy Dwight Harrison; it's all because of you.

Suddenly the conductor cried, all aboard, all aboard for Ivy Green. Buford was helped aboard the train with his luggage, and as the conductor shut the door, the old soldier played his trumpet, and the people cheered. It was quite simply the most amazing thing I have ever seen.

It crossed my mind momentarily; I wish Buford could see all of this. But then I remembered one of the first things I ever heard Buford say; there are more ways to see, other than with the eyes.

After we were settled into our seats, the train continued through the mountains of West Virginia. I felt a sense of adventure that I've never felt since that time. We had meals in the beautiful dining car, where everyone was exceptionally cordial and kind to Buford.

Through the night we took turns sleeping a while and then talking a while. Buford tried to explain to me what this trip meant to him.

He explained that we each have many moments in life some good, some bad. Quoting Scripture, Buford said each of us is given three scores, and 10 and the wise person will use their 70 years doing good for others. Buford quoted an ancient philosopher who said the unexamined life is not worth living

I now realize that Buford took every opportunity to teach me a valuable lesson about life. I think Buford would be proud that I'm telling his story and trying to inspire people to live with purpose as he taught me to do.

It's not the big moments and the applause a celebrity might receive, but it's the little things we do for people every day.

As morning broke the next day and we were drinking our coffee, I finally got the courage to ask Buford why this trip was so important to him. I said, are you still in love with Helen? Buford turned toward the window, and I don't know what he saw, but it was almost as if he had seen a scene from another world.

It was a striking moment, the first time I heard Buford say the word, God.

Buford said, Timothy, for God, so loved

Buford did not finish that sentence, but said, Timothy someday you will fall in love, get married and have children. You'll realize that there is nothing greater on this earth than the love between two people.

Buford

IVY GREEN, TUSCUMBIA, ALABAMA.

Buford

The story of Helen Keller and her lifelong instructor and friend, Anne Sullivan, is one of the most inspirational stories of all time.

It is almost incomprehensible even to try to imagine the process that these two people went through, with failures, of course, but accomplishments almost beyond belief.

Most of us can imagine at least a small degree not having eyesight we can also imagine the complete hearing loss.

As you have read earlier, as a child, I tried to imagine the world that my friend Buford lived in with no vision. But to be born without both vision and hearing is almost impossible to understand. One of the lessons that Buford taught me as a child was the importance of language, one of the greatest blessings of humankind. Because of his lack of vision, Buford appreciated proper language far more than the average person. Buford was educated, and a very intelligent human being and he could not imagine the pain, suffering, and devastation of being born into the world with no knowledge, not even understanding who or what you are.

The story of Anne Sullivan and Helen Keller is one of the greatest love stories of all time – not the romantic story – but the story of altruistic love. More should be said about Anne Sullivan, who went through hell to educate Helen Keller when she was a child. She gave her life in love and friendship to be Helen's teacher and companion through life.

The lives of these two courageous women are dramatized in the Broadway play and movie, *The Miracle Worker.*

Every summer, the play is reenacted several evenings during the summer by local producers and actors at Ivy Green.

Some of the truly great people, never receive the accolades they are due. After Buford and I spent a glorious day at Ivy green realizing the tremendous power for good that can come from the human heart, we were both inspired to reach out to people with our personal stories of inspiration, to make a difference by having passed this way.

I have waited until now to tell the story of my friend Buford, who of course has gone on that final journey, beyond the veil. As I write this story, I am an old man now. All those I have loved and did not always understand, are gone, but I still remember and reach out to them.

I'll never know what went through the mind of Buford on the day we spent at Ivy green, but it was one of the most wonderful days of my life, simply watching my friend Buford, walking through the grounds touching the bark on the old trees, walking the brick pathways and experiencing everything that had to do with Helen Keller's youth

The most touching moment came at the old water well pump where Anne Sullivan taught Helen Keller to say her first word,

WATER.

With his hand on the well-pump handle, Buford said, Timothy,

As water is to life, so love is to the soul.

THE MIRACLE

WORKER

LESSONS

FOR

LIFE

Buford

Buford always told me to play with good children and to make sure that my friends were from good families. People are not bad because they are born bad, but because of their parents, friends, and associates.

Buford told me that the best friendships and relationships are those in which each person makes the other person a better person.

Buford and I were friends, but I was only an elementary school kid. Buford had been to Harvard University. I know that he made a lasting impression on my life and helped me to be a better person, but I don't know if I contributed anything to his life or not. But I feel confident that he did learn something from me, though I know not what. But that, itself, is a valuable lesson that I learned from Buford and my father. There is always something to learn from another person even children.

It takes humility to respect all people and to learn from them, but Buford taught me that a truly wise person would respect, every individual, man, woman, and child. Remembering my time with Buford, near the end of my own life – or at least in the senior years, I have adopted this motto,

EVERYONE HAS A STORY TO TELL, AND EVERY STORY IS IMPORTANT

Life is sacred and holy. All creatures who breathe the air, even the mammals of the sea, and the animals of the earth, share one common thing—life.

Buford

In the beginning, I described the little apartment where Buford lived about the Central Café. I mentioned two things hanging on the wall, a photograph of Helen Keller and Buford's diploma from Harvard University. In that description, I failed to mention one thing: There was a small wooden cross.

Buford, with all the lessons he taught me, never mentioned religion or church.

I don't remember if Buford ever went to church or not. I have the feeling he did not,

Buford taught me the same thing that Jesus taught during his ministry, basically the golden rule, which is a part of every major religion in some form. Most everyone, either intuitively, or through teaching, or reading, knows the meaning of the Golden Rule. The lesson is this, love your neighbor and help them.

I mentioned seeing the little cross in Buford's apartment, because everything that he had was important to him, even though the items were few. And now that I think about it, I did see a book written in braille with the familiar title, *The Holy Bible.*

There seems to be one commonality among people my age, the seniors in society, and that is regret about not learning more from our parents, teachers, and the people we looked up to.

I can't begin to tell the number of times that I have thought about questions I would like to ask my father. If I could have just one afternoon, to sit down with my father and listen to his stories about his childhood and my grandparents, what a blessing that would be.

Most of my adult life I have wanted to write a book about my father and his early years. I remember some of the stories, but there's so much he could tell me. I have long thought that I would write a book about his stories, and call it, *The*

Teacher, Principle, Basketball Coach, and School Bus Driver.

Along with that same vein, I've often thought how nice it would be to have another chance to learn from Buford, the man with no eyes. Buford must've been about 15 years older than my father, who was born in 1900 and died 47 years ago. Based on the philosophies of the two men, there are some things that I hold sacrosanct about life.

The first thing I would like to ask Buford – what is the most important element of civilization? From the things he taught me, I'm sure he would agree that the nuclear family is indispensable to the well-being of any civilized society. The glory that was Rome, which lasted 1000 years, according to the historian Gibbons, began its decline with the destruction of the family. Our nation today seems to be on the Westward slope of decline, as the family appears less and less important in our culture. Statistics are available on the prison populations which show that the majority of those in prison did not have a father figure in their childhood.

If I could ask Buford today, what is the most important element of relationships, I'm quite positive that he would answer respect. I've never known of a truly great man – not just famous – but a truly good and great man, who did not respect all life and all people. I say all life for a specific reason because the truly great person respects not only people but mammals that breathe the same air we do. Edward Abbey, the environmental author, and activist said those who do not respect animals would eventually lose respect for human beings.

America today has become polarized to such an extent that people seem to have not only a lack of respect for each other but vitriol, even hatred for those of differing political persuasions. Buford would have a lot to say about education and learning in general.

It was a great challenge for him to finish his education at Harvard University while going blind. Part of his inspiration came from Helen Keller as well as other people who succeeded despite great personal challenges. I didn't learn as a child why Buford had to have his eyes removed. It breaks my heart when I think about it because I believe if he were living now that would not have been necessary. But the big blind man seemed to have accepted blindness and the loss of his eyes as his personal cross to bear, without complaint.

Despite the great challenges he faced, Buford was wise and well educated and well read. In thinking of things that Buford would list as important in life, at the top would be humility and kindness. I believe he would tell us today to never expect great things to come out of Washington, but for each of us to unite and make things better. I believe Buford would say a better world begins with you and me.

Finally, Buford would say, regardless of your station or position in life and the physical handicaps that you may have, live your life well.

A life that is not lived with purpose is a life wasted. Regardless of your ability and disabilities, find something that you can do and do well, that benefits others. Every story, remember, is important. Above all, remember the most important things in life are relationships. Try to make a difference by having been here.

Paso porAqui.

.

"Eyes are Useless When the mind is blind."

Amazing Grace

Amazing grace! How sweet the
sound,
That saved a wretch; like me!
I once was lost, but now am found,
 Was blind, but now I see.

'Twas grace that taught my heart
to fear,
And graces my fears relieved;
How precious did that grace
appear
The hour I first believed!

The Lord has promised good to
me,

His word my hope secures;

He will my shield and portion be

As long as life endures.

When we've been there ten

thousand years,

Bright shining as the sun,

We've no less days to sing God's

praise

Than when we first began.

- *Amazing Grace* John Newton

Author

Jerry W. Burns lives in Dallas, Texas, where he has a son and a daughter, and they each have a son and daughter. Jerry is an author, artist, former pastor, pilot, race car driver, and yacht designer and manufacturer. He was vice president of Burns-Craft Yachts.

Jerry studied philosophy at the University of Michigan and graduated from Abilene Christian University.

Buford

_____

www.ingramcontent.com/pod-product-compliance
Lightning Source LLC
Chambersburg PA
CBHW070552130626
46556CB00001B/132